Tales from Shakespeare

Hamlet

Rosencrantz and Guildenstern
Hamlet's friends

The Ghost of Hamlet's father
Former King of Denmark

Gertrude
Hamlet's mother,
Queen of Denmark

Polonius
The King's chief advisor

Gravedigger

Horatio
Hamlet's best friend

Ophelia
Polonius's daughter,
Hamlet's girlfriend

Hamlet
Prince of Denmark

King Claudius
Hamlet's uncle – his
father's brother – and
Gertrude's new husband

Laertes
Polonius's son

Timothy Knapman
Illustrated by Yaniv Shimony

The Castle and the Ghost

Act one

Horatio was tired and very, very cold.

He had been travelling for days to see his best friend, Prince Hamlet. They were students together at university in Germany, but a few weeks ago Hamlet had received terrible news. His father, the king of Denmark, had died. Hamlet raced home to Elsinore castle for the funeral, but Horatio hadn't heard from him since, and that worried him.

Horatio expected to see Hamlet the moment he arrived at the castle. Instead, he was met by Marcellus, the captain of the guard.

Marcellus said there was something Horatio had to see, and marched him straight up to the grim castle battlements.

Stay, illusion: If thou hast any sound or use of voice, Speak to me
– Horatio

"It's the middle of the night and it's freezing," Horatio complained. "Will you please tell me why you've brought me here?"

"You'll know soon enough, sir," Marcellus replied. "Look! Here it comes!"

The castle guards looked terrified and fell to the ground. Walking towards them, dressed from head to toe in armour, was a ghost! The ghost wore its visor up, so they could see its face. It was the ghost of the dead king, Hamlet's father! The ghost looked at them in silence, then disappeared.

"We must tell Hamlet!" said Horatio. "Perhaps the ghost will speak to him."

How weary, stale, flat, and unprofitable seem to me all the uses of this world!
– Hamlet

Prince Hamlet was sitting alone in the throne room. He had never thought he could be so sad. Was it only a few weeks since his father had died? So much had changed!

When Hamlet arrived home for the funeral, he found a new king already sitting on the throne: Claudius, his father's brother. Hamlet's father had been brave, noble and just. His uncle was lazy, greedy and sly.

But that wasn't what made Hamlet so sad.

No, he was sad because a week ago – scarcely a month after his father's death – his mother, Gertrude, had sat him down and said, "Your uncle and I are getting married." As if it was the most normal thing in the world!

After all the love his father had lavished on her. After all the tears she had cried at his funeral.

Hamlet thought everyone else in the castle would be upset, but no – they were all celebrating!

On the wedding day, they dressed up in their brightest party outfits. Only Hamlet still wore black mourning clothes.

Frailty, thy name is woman!
– Hamlet

Even now, long past midnight, the music from another celebration was still echoing through the castle.

Hamlet thought he must be going mad. He was so sad that he wanted to die. Something had gone very, very wrong in Denmark. If only he could put it right! But how?

"There you are!" cried Horatio. At once, the words pulled Hamlet out of his gloomy thoughts.

"Horatio!" he said. "My dearest friend!"

The time is out of joint. O cursed spite, that ever I was born to set it right!
— Hamlet

"I've missed you," said Horatio. Hamlet looked terrible. He was thin and pale, with black marks under his eyes. Horatio was right to have worried about him.

"But what have you come all this way for?" asked Hamlet. "Was it my father's funeral? Or my mother's wedding?"

"There wasn't much time between them, it's true," said Horatio.

"My uncle wanted to save money," Hamlet joked grimly.

"Any food that wasn't eaten at the funeral could be served up cold at the wedding." The smile died on his face and he gave a terrible sigh. "Oh, my poor father!"

"That's what I want to talk to you about," said Horatio. "Though you might not believe what I'm going to tell you..."

The next night it was even colder up on the battlements. As the castle clock struck twelve, the ghost rose out of the night mist. It beckoned to Hamlet and he followed, leaving Horatio behind.

Something is rotten in the state of Denmark
– Marcellus

When they were alone, the ghost turned to Hamlet.

"Listen to me," it rasped in a harsh voice. "I don't have long before I must go back to being punished for the evil things I did in my life."

"You never did anything evil, Father!" said Hamlet.

"Everyone does evil in this world," said the ghost, "and if you die without confessing your sins to God, you must suffer terrible punishment until you've paid for them all. Only then can you go to heaven."

"Oh poor ghost!" said Hamlet. There were tears in his eyes.

"Do you love me?" said the ghost.

"Of course I do, Father!" said Hamlet.

"Then avenge me," said the ghost, "because I was murdered."

"Murdered?" gasped Hamlet. "They told me you died because you were bitten by a poisonous snake!"

"No, my son," said the ghost. "My brother, Claudius, poured poison in my ear – and now he wears my crown."

I am thou father's spirit... Revenge his foul and most unnatural murder
– Ghost

"My uncle!" said Hamlet. "I knew it! Oh Father, I promise you that I will not rest until he is dead!"

Acting Mad

Act two

"**P**rince Hamlet will never marry you!"
Laertes was feeling anxious. He was supposed to be leaving that day for Paris but he was worried about his sister, Ophelia.

"Why not?" said Ophelia. "Am I too ugly?"

"Of course not!" said Laertes. "You're beautiful! But Hamlet is a prince, and princes marry princesses, not people like us! I couldn't bear to see him break your heart."

"You don't know what you're talking about," said Ophelia. She loved Hamlet with all her heart, but she was concerned about him. He'd been miserable since his father died, and lately he'd been acting very oddly. Maybe Laertes was right after all...

Before she could say any more, in walked their father, Polonius, the king's advisor.

"There you are, Laertes!" said Polonius. "If you don't get a move on, your ship will leave without you!"

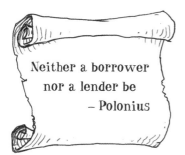

Neither a borrower nor a lender be
– Polonius

"Of course, Father," said Laertes, picking up his bag. "A few words of advice for when you're away," said Polonius. "Don't make friends with anyone until you know that you can trust them. Don't borrow money, or lend it either. And try not to get into fights. I know what you're like – but if you can't stop yourself, make sure you win!

Last of all: be true to yourself – that way you can't be false to anyone else."

"I will do as you say, Father," said Laertes. "Goodbye."

"Goodbye, my son," said Polonius.

"Goodbye, Ophelia," said Laertes. "Remember what I said."

Polonius waited until Laertes was gone before he asked Ophelia, "What was that about?"

"Prince Hamlet," said Ophelia.

"Yes," said Polonius. "We're all worried about him..."

King Claudius was pacing up and down the throne room.

"What's the matter, my love?" asked Queen Gertrude.

"It's that son of yours..." said Claudius. "Ever since Hamlet's friend Horatio came to stay, he's been acting very strangely:

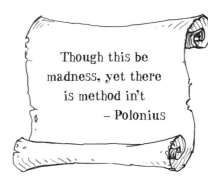

Though this be madness, yet there is method in't
– Polonius

wandering around the place, talking to himself – talking nonsense most of the time!"

"He's sad about his father," said Gertrude.

"My brother?" said Claudius. "But he died weeks ago!"

Gertrude shook her head. She loved her new husband but he could be heartless.

"He's in love with Ophelia," said Claudius, "and love makes people do strange things, but is that all?" He took a gulp of wine. "You don't think he's plotting to get rid of me, do you?"

"Of course not, my love," said Gertrude.

"I'm not so sure," said Claudius. "So I've ordered a couple of his friends, Rosencrantz and Guildenstern, to come and visit him.

Madness in great
ones must not
unwatched go
– Claudius

He has no secrets from them. They'll tell me what's really going on."

Hamlet wasn't just acting oddly, he was pretending to be mad. The ghost's words had shaken him, but the more he thought about them, the more he doubted them. What if the ghost wasn't his father after all? What if it was a demon, sent by the devil to trick him into killing his uncle? If Claudius was innocent and Hamlet killed him, Hamlet would go to hell.

No, Hamlet needed more proof that his uncle was guilty – but how was he going to get it? He needed time and space to think, and the madder he acted, the more people avoided him.

Hamlet was alone
in his room when
there was a knock
at the door.

He opened
it, and gasped at
the sight of the
two young men
standing there.

"Rosencrantz
and Guildenstern?"
said Hamlet. He was
delighted to see his
friends, but he remembered
that he had to act oddly.
"What brings you to this prison?"

"Is this a prison?" asked Rosencrantz.
"I thought it was a castle."

"Denmark is a prison to me,"
said Hamlet.

"You're very gloomy," said Guildenstern.
"What's the matter?"

Guildenstern was trying to sound jokey and relaxed, but there was a strange sound to his voice. Hamlet couldn't put his finger on it, but he knew something was wrong.

"Did my uncle the king tell you to come here?" he asked.

"Of course not!" said Rosencrantz.

"You're our friend and we missed you!" said Guildenstern.

But Hamlet could tell he was lying. His heart sank. Now there were two more people he could never trust again...

"You can tell my uncle that I'm sad," said Hamlet. "I don't know why, but everything in this beautiful world seems worthless to me."

There is nothing either good or bad, but thinking makes it so
– Hamlet

Rosencrantz and Guildenstern looked at each other. The king wouldn't be satisfied with that! They had to keep Hamlet talking.

"Here's something to cheer you up," said Rosencrantz. "A party of actors has just arrived at the castle."

"Yes," said Guildenstern, "we know how much you like actors. They're going to put on a play here tonight."

"Actors?" said Hamlet – and suddenly he had a brilliant idea! "That is good news!"

Hamlet always enjoyed the actors' visits to the castle, but now he knew that they were also the answer to his problem.

He pushed past Rosencrantz and Guildenstern and ran down the great stone staircase into the castle courtyard.

The actors were unloading the costumes
and scenery for the play. Hamlet recognized
the noble-looking actor who played kings,
and the funny-looking one who made
everyone laugh.

"My friends, welcome to Elsinore!"
Hamlet cried.

The actors stopped what they were
doing and bowed to the prince.

"Have you decided what you're
going to perform tonight?"
Hamlet asked.

"There's a play I know that would be perfect."

"We are at your service," said the noble-looking actor.

Hamlet's plan was this: the actors would perform a play in which a king is killed by his brother. Hamlet would study his uncle's face as he watched the play.

If Claudius got angry, it would be because of his guilt.

Then Hamlet would know

for sure that Claudius had killed his father.

And then Hamlet would kill him.

The play's the thing wherein I'll catch the conscience of the king!
— Hamlet

The Play's the Thing

Act three

Hamlet's good mood didn't last. He had a plan, but that wasn't enough to make him forget his problems.

His father had been murdered, and so many of the people Hamlet loved had taken the side of the man who murdered him.

Soon, Hamlet was gloomier than he had ever been.

"Perhaps it's better to die than to go on living in a world like this," he thought. "Except that death might be worse! They say death is like going to sleep – but what if that sleep is full of nightmares?

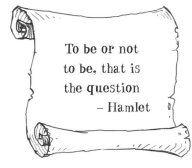

To be or not to be, that is the question
– Hamlet

We don't know,
so we stay alive
because we're too
scared to find out."

Hamlet heard
footsteps behind
him and turned
round.
    "Oh, thank
heavens it's
you, Ophelia,"
he began.
    He felt so
lonely. He wanted
to tell her that he loved her, that he was
sorry he'd been acting so strangely.
    But before he had the chance,
Ophelia held up her hand to silence him.
    "There's something I want to say,"
she said coldly. "I don't love you any
more, Hamlet."

Ophelia felt terrible saying the words, but her father had commanded it. He said Hamlet's love for her had driven the prince mad. Ophelia would do anything to help Hamlet, but she felt as if her heart was breaking.

Hamlet was stunned. Why on earth would Ophelia say that? And then he noticed something. In the shadows on the other side of the room, he saw a movement. He could just make out two men hiding and listening – they were spying on him! He looked closer. It was Claudius and Polonius.

They had told Ophelia
to do this, and she
had said yes!
The pain went
through Hamlet
like a knife.
"If my love
isn't good
enough for
you," he said

Get thee to a
nunnery
– Hamlet

angrily, "you should go and
become a nun!" He turned his
back on her and walked off.
Ophelia wanted to call him back, to
explain everything, to tell him the truth.
But she realized it was too late.

The banqueting hall of Elsinore castle had
been turned into a theatre for the night. At
one end, the actors had built a stage. The
rest of the room was crammed with people
who couldn't wait for the show to start.

There was a fanfare and the king and queen entered and took their seats. Everyone fell silent as the play began.

Hamlet made sure he could see his uncle's face. He didn't turn away, not even when the fat king kissed his mother's hand. How Hamlet hated that!

At last, the actors reached the important part of the play. The actor playing the king lay down to sleep. Hamlet noticed that Claudius had stopped smiling. Back on stage, the wife gave the king's brother a bottle of poison. Claudius dropped his wine cup as he watched the brother creep over to the sleeping king and pour the poison into his ear.

Claudius sprang to his feet. "How dare you?" he roared. "Stop this play at once!"

The actors looked up in terror as Claudius stormed out of the room.

So it was true! Claudius had murdered Hamlet's father! Hamlet drew his sword and raced after him.

O, my offence is rank, it smells to heaven
– Claudius

Hamlet found Claudius in the castle chapel kneeling in front of the altar. Hamlet crept up behind him and lifted his sword to strike.

He was about to bring it down on the murderer's head when he realized something. Hamlet's father hadn't had a chance to confess his sins to God before he died, and that's why he was being punished after death.

If Hamlet killed Claudius now, while he was praying, Claudius would go straight to heaven. What kind of revenge would that be?

Hamlet put down his sword.

He would wait until the king was doing something greedy or selfish – which was most of the time – and then, before he could say he was sorry, Hamlet would kill him and send him straight to hell.

Hamlet left the chapel. There was someone else he needed to talk to.

Hamlet's mother, Gertrude, was in her bedroom with Polonius.

"What is going on?" she asked. She was very upset.

"I have no idea, your Majesty," said Polonius, "but I saw Prince Hamlet talking to the actors this afternoon. This is all his fault."

They could hear running feet outside.

Polonius peered through a crack in the door.

"It's Hamlet, your Majesty," he said. "See if you can find out what he's up to. I'll hide behind that tapestry over there and listen."

Polonius disappeared just as Hamlet burst in, sword in hand.

"What are you doing?" said Gertrude. "You've upset the king!"

"*I've* upset the king?" cried Hamlet. "You're the one who married his brother!"

"Your father is dead, Hamlet," said Gertrude. "Claudius is king now – and he's also my husband."

"How could you do it, Mother?" said Hamlet angrily.

"Put your sword away," said Gertrude. "You're frightening me!"

"Guards! Quickly! The queen is in danger!" cried Polonius from behind the tapestry.

"Is that the king?" asked Hamlet. "How did he sneak in here?"

Quick as a flash, Hamlet spun round and stabbed his sword through the curtain. There was a scream and Polonius fell out onto the floor, dead.

"Oh Hamlet, what have you done?" cried Gertrude.

"Nothing compared to you!" said Hamlet. "I didn't kill a king and marry his murderer!"

"What are you talking about?" said Gertrude.

Hamlet picked up Polonius's body and started to drag it out of the room.

"Confess your sins to God, Mother," said Hamlet, "while you still have a chance."

A bloody deed. Almost as bad, good mother, As kill a king and marry with his brother
— Hamlet

Grief and Vengeance

Act four

Gertrude was still shaking when Claudius found her.

"My darling! Are you all right?" he said as he held her close.

"What are we going to do about Hamlet?" Gertrude sobbed.

"You leave him to me..." said Claudius.

Less than an hour later, Hamlet stood before Claudius, surrounded by guards. His eyes glittered with hatred.

How dangerous it is that this man goes loose!
– Claudius

"If it was up to me, you'd be in the dungeons, charged with murder," said Claudius. "But your mother begged me to spare you, so I'm sending you to England. Rosencrantz and Guildenstern have agreed to go with you."

"Here." He handed Rosencrantz a letter. "This is for the king of England. You know what it says. Now take him away."

Hamlet was furious as they marched him down to the harbour. If only that silly old fool Polonius hadn't interfered!

As his ship sailed for England, Hamlet was still wondering how to kill Claudius.

O, from this time forth
My thoughts be bloody or be nothing worth
– Hamlet

The moment Laertes heard that his father, Polonius, had been murdered, he rushed back to Denmark, bent on revenge.

He pushed past the guards at the castle gate and strode angrily inside.

Claudius sprang to his feet. "My poor boy!" he exclaimed. "I cannot tell you how sorry I am."

"Never mind that!" barked Laertes. "Where is Hamlet? I want him dead!"

"I have taken care of him," said Claudius.

Let come what comes, only I'll be reveng'd Most thoroughly for my father
– Laertes

He didn't have a chance to explain what he meant. From outside the throne room, they heard a voice, cracked by sorrow and madness, singing.

"I know that voice, don't I?" said Laertes. "Oh please don't tell me it's..."

But before he could finish his sentence, his sister Ophelia appeared, singing.

Her bright eyes were dark with misery. The shock of her father's death at the hands of the man she loved had broken her. She was quite mad.

"Ophelia!" Laertes cried.

Ophelia had a bunch of dead flowers in her hands. She walked around the room, handing them out.

"There's rosemary – that's to remember him by. Here are pansies – those are for thoughts for the dead. This is rue – for all of our regrets."

She gave the last of her flowers to Laertes. She was looking at him, but he wasn't sure she even knew who he was.

"I'm sorry," said Ophelia. "I have to pick some more flowers." She gave a little curtsey to the king and queen, then left.

Claudius could see that Laertes was fighting back tears.

"Come into my chamber," he said. He knew Laertes would hate for anyone to see him cry, and besides, they had something secret to talk about.

"I have to kill Hamlet!" roared Laertes when they were alone. "I don't care about going to hell – I must have my vengeance!"

"If he ever comes back to Denmark, you can kill him," said Claudius. "But if things have gone according to plan, he should be dead already."

Revenge at Last

Act five

Hamlet didn't trust Rosencrantz and Guildenstern. As they slept on the ship, he sneaked into their cabin. There he found the letter from Claudius.

"To his Royal Majesty, the king of England," it said, "Prince Hamlet is a dangerous madman. Please **kill** him as soon as you read this letter."

Hamlet was very angry. His so-called 'friends' were taking him to his death!

Taking care not to wake them, Hamlet rewrote the letter.

Now it said: "Rosencrantz and Guildenstern are dangerous madmen. Please kill them."

He put the letter back where he found it and was slipping out of the cabin when there was a cry from above.

"Pirates!" shouted the lookout. "All hands on deck!"

But it was too late. The pirate ship was already alongside theirs, and the pirates jumped aboard, their cutlasses flashing in the moonlight.

After a few short minutes of fighting, they took control of the ship. "Take all their gold and jewels," roared the pirate captain.

"And who do we have here? Prince Hamlet!
He'll fetch a good ransom if we take him
back to Denmark!"

The pirates took Hamlet back to
their ship. He watched from its deck as
Rosencrantz and Guildenstern sailed on
to England, and certain death.

When Hamlet got back to
Denmark, he went straight
to see Horatio. Horatio could
scarcely believe Hamlet's story
of what had happened at sea.

"So what are you going
to do now?" asked Horatio.

"I suppose I'll go back to the castle
and finish this dreadful business," said
Hamlet wearily.

Hamlet had only been away for a few
days, but he seemed much older somehow.
The rage had gone out of him. Instead,
Horatio saw only a deep sadness.

As the two friends walked towards Elsinore castle, their route took them through a graveyard. They were surprised to hear the gravedigger singing happily.

They were even more surprised when a skull came flying up out of the grave he was digging!

"Oops, sorry gents!" said the gravedigger with a smile. "There's not enough room in this graveyard. Sometimes we have to dig up one of our guests to make room for a new arrival."

Hamlet picked up the skull and turned it over in his hands.

"Whose skull is this?" he asked.

"That's the old king's jester," said the gravedigger. "His name was Yorick."

"Is this really Yorick?" said Hamlet. "I remember him! He was so funny. Where are your jokes now, Yorick?" Hamlet shook his head. "All gone."

Alas, poor Yorick! I knew him, Horatio, a fellow of infinite jest
– Hamlet

"Who are you making room for?" said Horatio.

"A poor young lady," said the gravedigger. "She was picking flowers by the riverbank, they say. Only she was a bit soft in the head so she fell in and drowned."

"What was her name?" asked Hamlet.

"Ophelia, sir," said the gravedigger. "Look! Here she comes."

It was a small procession. Laertes, Gertrude and Claudius walked in front of the coffin, which was carried by castle guards.

Sweets to the sweet. Farewell.
– Gertrude

"Ophelia, my love! No!" cried Hamlet and he ran towards the coffin.

"You!" shrieked Laertes when he saw him. "This is your fault! You killed our father and drove my sister to madness!"

"I had no idea," said Hamlet. He was devastated. "Forgive me, please. I never meant for this to happen."

He put his hand on Laertes' shoulder, but Laertes shoved him away angrily.

"This is no place for fighting," said Claudius. "I have an idea! Tonight Hamlet and Laertes will have a chance to settle their differences – when they fight a duel!"

The duel was to be held in the banqueting hall at the castle. A small crowd gathered to watch the two men fight.

As he took his place, Horatio couldn't help worrying about Hamlet. Duels weren't serious swordfights. No one was supposed to get badly hurt, but it was clear that Laertes meant to kill Hamlet!

"Silence for the king!" cried one of the guards.

Claudius rose to his feet.

"Before we start," he said, "I want one thing understood. Whoever wins tonight, that will be the end of any quarrel between you. Do you agree?"

"We do," said Hamlet and Laertes together, and they shook hands.

"Good," said Claudius. "Now choose your weapons."

A guard appeared, carrying two swords. Under his breath, Claudius whispered to Laertes, "Choose the one on the left. The blade has poison on it. One scratch and Prince Hamlet is dead!"

Laertes did as he was told.

"Begin!" shouted the king.

Hamlet fought much better than Horatio was expecting. He rushed at Laertes, cutting and slicing.

"Ouch!" cried Laertes. His cheek was bleeding.

"First blood to Hamlet!" cried Osric, the referee.

Claudius looked worried. "Well done, Hamlet!" he called. "Have a drink to celebrate!"

Claudius poured Hamlet a cup of wine.

"I'll have it later," said Hamlet. "Come on, Laertes. Let's start again."

A hit, a very palpable hit!
 – Osric

"I'll drink it," said Gertrude. "To my son, may he prove victorious!"

"Gertrude, no!" said Claudius, but before he could stop her, she had drained the cup.

"What's the matter?" she asked.

Claudius said nothing. It was too late. The wine was poisoned as well.

"Begin!" shouted Claudius.

Again, Hamlet and Laertes fought. This time, Laertes managed to cut Hamlet's shoulder with his poisoned sword. Hamlet roared with pain and knocked the sword out of Laertes' hand.

Laertes scrambled to get his sword back, but Hamlet jumped on him. As they scuffled, Hamlet lost his sword and grabbed Laertes' weapon instead!

Laertes picked up Hamlet's sword and they fought on.

Laertes tried desperately to avoid the poisoned blade, but it was no good. Hamlet drove it into Laertes' arm.

"Argh!" screamed Gertrude.

"Mother!" said Hamlet. "What's the matter?"

"The drink was poisoned!" Gertrude croaked, grabbing her throat.

"Gertrude, I'm sorry!" cried Claudius, but she was already dead.

"That sword is poisoned too," said Laertes. "You and I have only moments to live, Hamlet."

"Then I will put them to good use," said Hamlet. "Murderer!" he cried, leaping at his uncle and stabbing him with the poisoned sword.

Hamlet, thou art slain...
In thee there is not
half an hour's life...
the king's to blame.
    – Laertes

Claudius screamed and fell to the ground, dead. Hamlet dropped the sword. He could already feel its poison beginning to work on him. He stumbled into Horatio's arms.

"Oh my friend," Hamlet said. "At last, I know what it feels like to have my revenge!"

Hamlet, Prince of Denmark, smiled sadly one last time, then the life went out of him.

Horatio hugged his dead body. Crying softly, he whispered, "Good night, sweet prince, and flights of angels sing thee to thy rest."

The end

The rest is
silence
– Hamlet

Consultant: Dr Tamsin Badcoe
Editors: Ruth Symons and Carly Madden
Designer: Andrew Crowson
QED Project Designer: Rachel Lawston
Editorial Director: Victoria Garrard
Art Director: Laura Roberts-Jensen

First published in the UK in 2015 by
QED Publishing
A Quarto Group company
The Old Brewery
6 Blundell Street
London N7 9BH

A catalogue record for this book is available from
the British Library.

ISBN 978 1 78493 001 1

Printed in China

www.qed-publishing.co.uk